THIS WALKER BOOK BELONGS TO:

For Lorcan and Augusta
Born 6th July 2005 ♡♡

A big thank you to everyone
at Walker Books, especially
David and Audrey

First published 2007 by Walker Books Ltd
87 Vauxhall Walk, London SE11 5HJ

10 9 8 7 6 5 4 3 2 1

©2007 Jessica Spanyol

The right of Jessica Spanyol to be identified as author/illustrator
of this work has been asserted by her in accordance with the
Copyright, Designs and Patents Act 1988

This book has been typeset in LN Spanyol

Printed in Singapore

British Library Cataloguing in Publication Data:
a catalogue record for this book is available from the British Library

ISBN 978-1-84428-024-7 (hb)
ISBN 978-1-4063-0733-7 (pb)

www.walkerbooks.co.uk

Little Neighbours

of Sunnyside Street

Jessica Spanyol

WALKER BOOKS

AND SUBSIDIARIES

LONDON • BOSTON • SYDNEY • AUCKLAND

Welcome to Sunnyside Street

Let's meet some of the *Little Neighbours* who live in Sunnyside Street. They have lots of fun things to do today.

Ian and his little sister, *Baby Jade*, live at number 4. **Ian** really likes playing with *Baby Jade* and he is very good at it.

Kelly lives at number 5. It is a lovely house, but sometimes it gets a bit messy.

The Bugs live at number 6. It is a funny
little house with lots and lots of garages.

Philip lives at number 7. Today he is busy collecting cardboard boxes.

Little Neighbours
at number 4

Music
with Ian

Ian really likes music and he is very good at it. Here he is getting out his instruments: a xylophone, a flute and a drum. Ian's little sister, *Baby Jade*, loves the way Ian plays her favourite song.

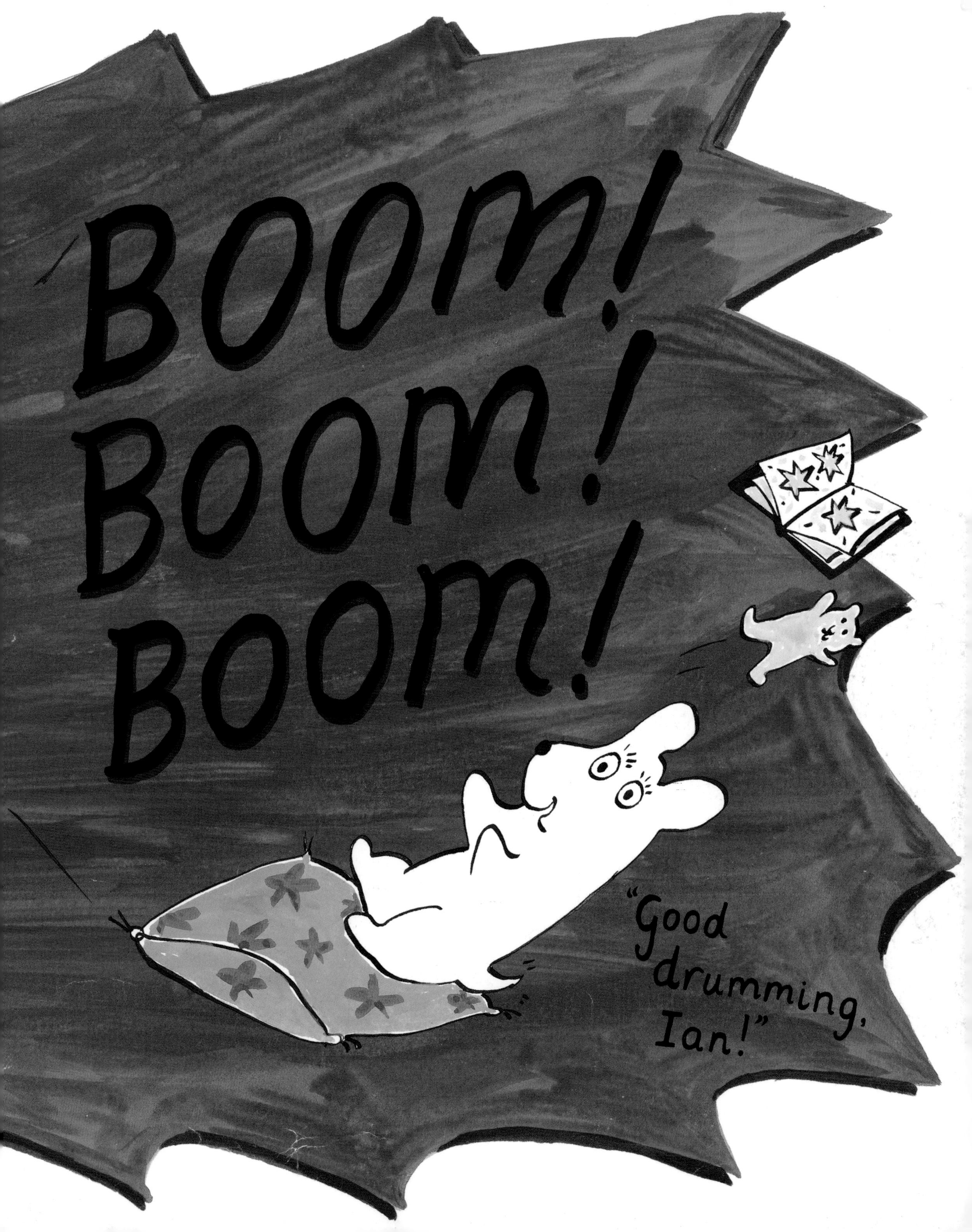
BOOM!
BOOM!
BOOM!
"Good drumming, Ian!"

Driving with the Bugs

All the Bugs are out driving in the backyard.
All the Bugs like driving.

Tate likes driving his vintage car.

Keith likes driving his sizzling Firebug.

The Triplets like driving their open-top car.

Mr Thornton-Jones likes giving his friends a ride in his Beetle.

Jo-Jo likes driving her van – she painted the flowers herself.

Stacie likes driving her classy car.

Bob likes driving his bubble car.

Giorgio likes driving his racing car.

Clemence likes driving his tiny yellow car.

Pauline and the girls like driving their Jeep.

And most of all they love to ...

bump and bash!

Making Things
with Philip

Philip likes making things.
Today he needs:

1 cardboard box
1 teddy bear
1 pair of scissors
1 pot of paint
1 brush

sticky tape /
pens / pencils

"Cut one big hole in the box and paint
some stars like this," says Philip.

"Then put the box over your head and ...

Zoom, zoom, zoom,
we're going to the moon.
5, 4, 3, 2, 1...
BLAST OFF!"

Messy Play
with Kelly

Little Neighbours

at number 5

Kelly is playing in her room. She really likes making a big mess. Here comes Mum, who wants to help Kelly tidy up.

"Books on here, darling," says Mum.

"Let's hang some clothes up. Good girl, Kelly, love."

"And all the toys in the box."

"That's nice and tidy. Now, I'll just get a coffee. Back in a minute..."

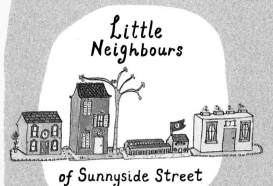

Little
Neighbours

of Sunnyside Street

Reading

Philip likes reading his song book.

"Teddy bear, teddy bear,
in your box.
Teddy bear, teddy bear,
tucked in tight.
Teddy bear, teddy bear,
turn out the light.
Teddy bear, teddy bear,
say
goodnight!"

SONG BOOK

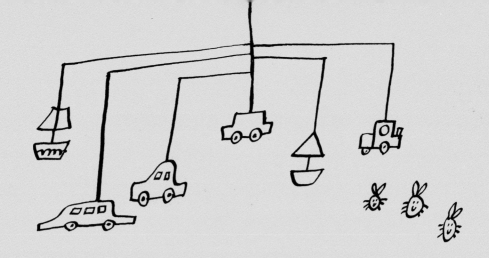

The Bugs like reading books about driving.

"All aboard the bug train, here we go!

Clickety clack, Clickety clack, Clickety clack."

Kelly likes reading
lots of books.

Ian likes reading
and he is very good at it.
Ian's little sister, *Baby Jade*,
loves the way Ian reads her
favourite book.

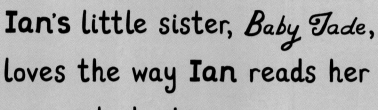

"Once upon a time there was a farm.
And on that farm there was:

One tiny brown mouse,

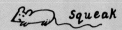 squeak

two fluffy white lambs,
 baa
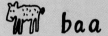 baa

three sleepy little kittens,
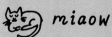 miaow
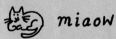 miaow
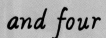 miaow

and four

very noisy

  ducks ..."

QUACK!

QUACK!

QUACK!

More Driving
with the Bugs

Here are **the Bugs** again, out driving in their backyard.

The Triplets like driving their milk lorry.

Keith likes driving his diesel train.

Mr Thornton-Jones likes giving his friends a ride in his bus.

Jo-Jo likes driving her tractor – she painted the flowers herself.

Bob likes driving his moped.

Stacie likes driving Classy Lady.

Pauline and the girls like driving their steam train.

Tate likes driving his skip truck. The skip is full of mud and stuff.

Giorgio likes driving his bulldozer.

Clemence likes driving his ambulance.

But most of all the Bugs love to ...

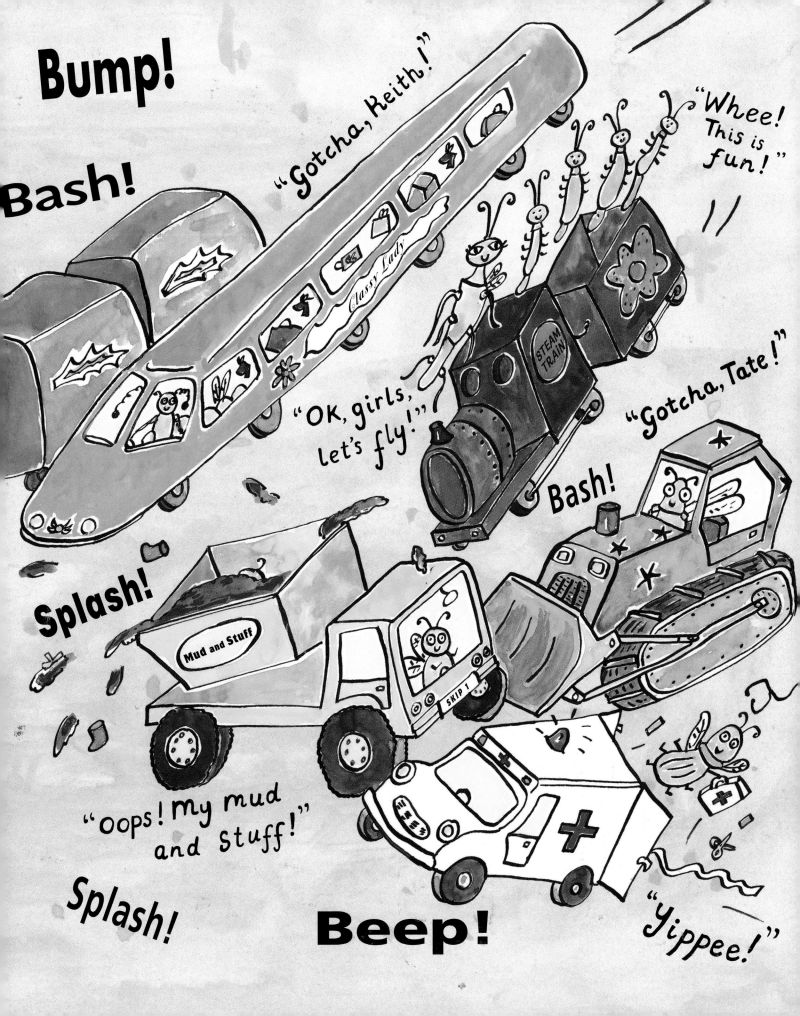

Little
Neighbours

at number 4

Painting
with Ian

Ian really likes painting and he is very good at it. Here he is getting all his paints ready.

Ian's little sister, *Baby Jade*, is going to watch **Ian** paint. *Baby Jade* likes lots of colours, but **black** is her favourite.

"A blob of red and a touch of green," says **Ian**.

"Now a dab of yellow and a smidgen of blue. And finally..."

More Making Things
with Philip

Here's Philip again, making something else.

Now he needs:

1 cardboard box
2 broom handles
2 bits of card cut into shapes like this:

some sticky tape

"Stick this here and this here," says Philip.

"Then step inside and ..."

Row, row, row your boat
Gently down the stream.
Merrily, Merrily,
Merrily, Merrily,
Life is but a dream."

More Messy Play
with Kelly

Kelly is getting out all her bits and bobs in the living room. She is going to make **Ian** a card. Here comes Dad, who wants to help keep things tidy.

"Let's put all your bits and bobs and sticking things on your table and some newspaper on the floor."

"Put your apron on, Kelly, love," says Dad.

"That's nice and tidy, darling. Now, I'm just going to let the cat in. Back in a minute..."

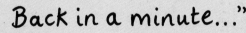

at number 4

Cooking
with Ian

Ian really likes cooking and he is really good at it.

Here he is getting out all the ingredients to make a cake.

Ian's little sister, *Baby Jade*, loves the way Ian cooks.

"A little bit of sugar and some flour."

"Then crack some eggs, add a pinch of salt and one jug of water. Then give the whole thing a really good ..."

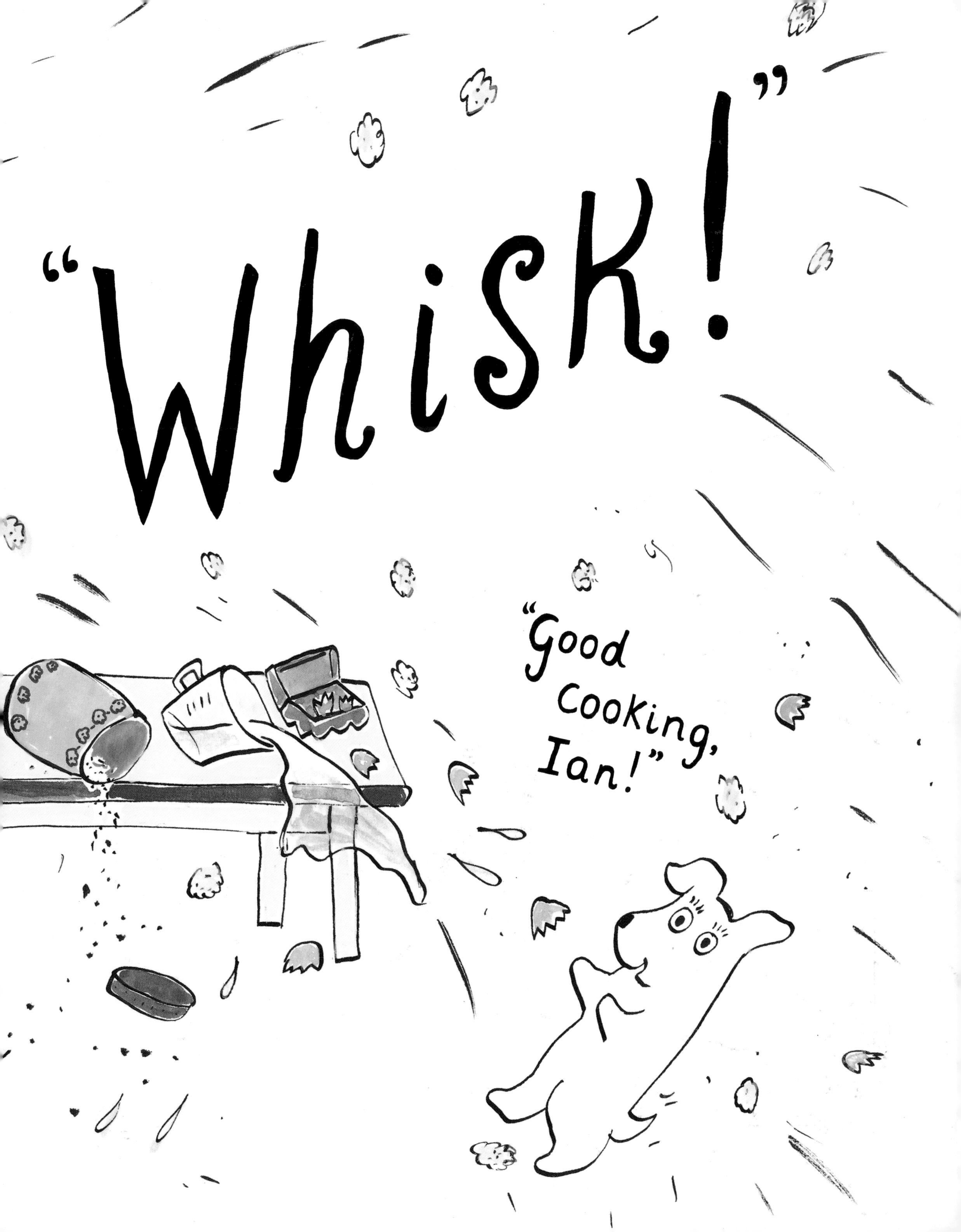
"Whisk!"
"Good cooking, Ian!"

Little
Neighbours

of Sunnyside Street

Partytime!

All the *Little Neighbours* are in **Ian's** garden for a party. **Ian** really likes parties and he is very good at them. He has put up lots of colourful balloons, made some delicious food and here he is putting on some party music.

Little
Neighbours

of Sunnyside Street

Sleeping

It has been a very busy day in Sunnyside Street.
But now it's time for sleeping.

Night-night, **Tate**.

Night-night, **Keith**.

Night-night, **Triplets**.

Night-night, **Stacie**.

Night-night,
Clemence.

Night-night,
Pauline and the girls.

Night-night, **Jo-Jo**.

Night-night, **Mr Thornton-Jones**
and friends.

Night-night, *Giorgio*.

Night-night, **Bob**.

Night-night,
Ian.

Night-night,
Baby Jade.

WALKER BOOKS is the world's leading
independent publisher of children's books.
Working with the best authors and illustrators
we create books for all ages, from babies
to teenagers – books your child will
grow up with and always remember. So…

FOR THE BEST CHILDREN'S BOOKS,
LOOK FOR THE BEAR